Alexa the Fashion Reporter Fairy

Special thanks to Narinder Dhami

ISBN 978-0-545-48487-9

Previously published as *Fashion Fairies #4: Alexa the Fashion Editor Fairy* by Orchard U.K. in 2012.

12 11 10 9 8 7 6 5 4 3 2 1 13 14 15 16 17 18/0

Printed in China 68

This edition first printing, July 2013

Alexa the Fashion Reporter Fairy

by Daisy Meadows

SCHOLASTIC INC.

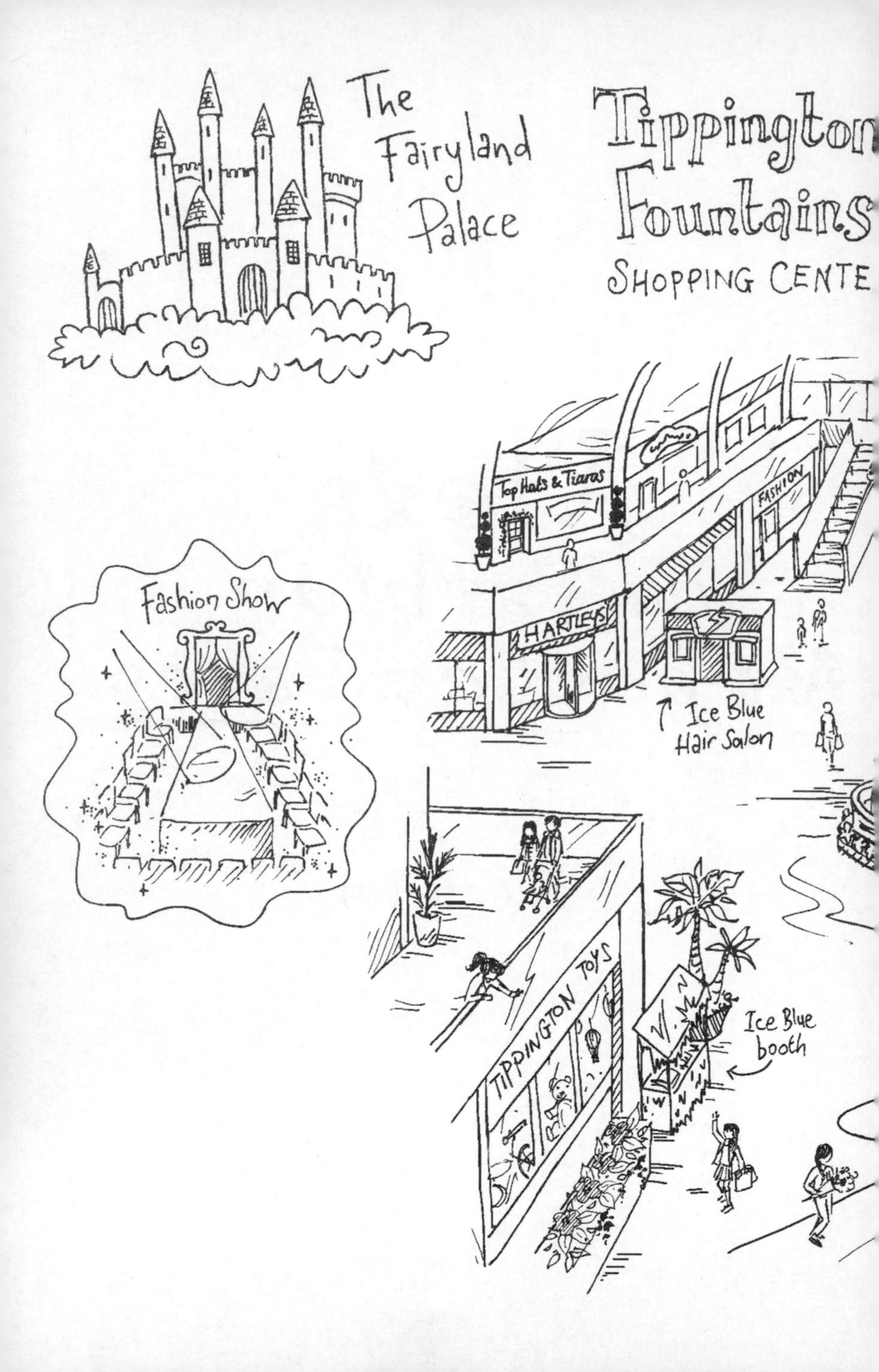
The Fairyland Palace
Tippington Fountains
SHOPPING CENTE
Top Hats & Tiaras
FASHION
HARTLEYS
Ice Blue Hair Salon
Fashion Show
TIPPINGTON TOYS
Ice Blue booth

Jack Frost's Ice Castle
Up to the Roof Garden Café
ELEVATOR
Finishing Touch
COMFY FEET
Ice cream parlor
WINTER WOOLIES
Beautiful YOU!
SNIP & CLIP
Central fountain
PRESS
Press booth
Bath Bliss

I'm the king of designer fashion,
Looking stylish is my passion.
Ice Blue's the name of my fashion line,
The designs are fabulous and they're all mine!

Some people think my clothes are odd,
But I will get the fashion world's nod.
Fashion Fairy magic will make my dream come true –
Soon everyone will wear Ice Blue!

Contents

"What should we call our fashion magazine, Rachel?" Kirsty asked, tapping her pencil thoughtfully on her sketch pad. "I can't think of a good title!"

The girls were in the beautiful landscaped park that surrounded the new Tippington Fountains Shopping Center, an enormous building made of chrome

and glass. Kirsty had come to stay with Rachel for the school break, and Mrs. Walker had taken them to the grand opening of Tippington Fountains earlier that week. Yesterday, Rachel and Kirsty had attended a workshop for the design competition at the shopping mall. The girls had enjoyed it so much, they'd decided to create their own fashion magazine! They were sitting on a picnic blanket on a soft carpet of red, yellow, and orange autumn leaves with their sketch pads and colored pencils.

Rachel was finishing a design for a T-shirt. "I'm not sure," she replied, glancing up as more leaves drifted down from the trees above them. "*Fashion for Girls*?"

"How about *Fantastic Fashions*?" suggested Rachel's dad. He was sitting nearby on a park bench, reading a newspaper.

“*Fabulous Fashions*?” Kirsty said, then shook her head. “No, that’s not special enough. What about *Fashion Magic*?”

“Perfect!” Rachel said with a grin. She held up her sketch pad to show Kirsty her T-shirt design. The T-shirt was bright orange with TIPPINGTON FOUNTAINS written in gold and red letters across the front. Between the words, Rachel had added a drawing of the spectacular fountains that were in the middle of the shopping mall. “I based the colors on the autumn leaves,” Rachel added.

"I think that should be our front cover," Kirsty said, admiring the design. "And I want to interview you about the workshop we went to yesterday, and then I'll write an article for the magazine." Kirsty cleared her throat and held a pretend microphone in front of Rachel. "So, Rachel," she said, "tell me what you did at the workshop yesterday."

"I wanted to make something really colorful, so I painted a rainbow on my jeans," Rachel explained.

"And how does it feel to be one of the competition

winners who will be modeling in the charity fashion show at the end of the week?" asked Kirsty.

Rachel burst out laughing. "Well, you should know," she pointed out. "You were one of the competition winners, too! Your flowy scarf dress was *gorgeous*."

"Girls," called Mr. Walker from the bench, "you might be interested in this for your magazine." He handed over an insert that had been inside his newspaper.

Rachel and Kirsty stared at the glossy flyer. The headline was *Be Cool as Ice in*

These Hot New Designs from ICE BLUE! The clothes in the photo were all ice-blue, and they looked strange. There was a jacket with only one sleeve, and a pair of pants with one short leg and one long leg. There was also a sweater knit from strips of blue plastic, and a pair of socks with holes instead of toes.

The girls exchanged horrified glances. They knew very well that Ice Blue was the fashion label created by the one and only Jack Frost!

On the day the shopping mall opened, the girls had been thrilled when their old

friend Phoebe the Fashion Fairy had invited them to Fairyland for a fashion show. The show had been organized by Phoebe's helpers, the seven Fashion Fairies. The Fashion Fairies looked after all the fashion in both the human and fairy worlds. But the event had hardly begun when Jack Frost and his goblins crashed the show, modeling their own crazy blue outfits. Jack Frost announced that soon everyone, humans and fairies alike, would be wearing his Ice Blue clothes. To help him achieve his goal, Jack Frost and his goblins had stolen the Fashion Fairies' magical objects. Then they had whisked them away to the Tippington Fountains mall.

"Jack Frost is determined to make *everyone* wear his silly blue clothes!"

Rachel murmured to Kirsty. "I just hope we can stop him."

"We've managed to find three of the Fashion Fairies' magic objects so far," Kirsty reminded her. "Let's hope we find the others before the charity fashion show at the end of the week."

Rachel nodded and brushed aside a scarlet leaf that had landed on her sketch pad. There weren't many leaves on the trees now, Rachel noticed, watching more float slowly to the ground. Soon it would be winter. . . .

A flash of light above her head suddenly caught Rachel's attention.

Another leaf, sparkling in the autumn sunshine, was drifting slowly down. *Leaves don't sparkle*, Rachel thought, her heart beating faster. *But fairies do!*

Quickly, Rachel pointed out the sparkling leaf to Kirsty.

"Oh!" Kirsty whispered. "Could it be?"

Rachel held a finger to her lips and pointed at her dad. Mr. Walker was focused on reading his newspaper and hadn't noticed a thing, so the girls rushed across the grass toward the falling leaf. They cupped their hands together, and the leaf landed lightly on their outstretched palms. But it wasn't a leaf at all — it was a tiny, sparkly fairy! Her long, shiny blond hair hung in a braid over one shoulder. She wore a blue dress with a Peter Pan collar, knee-high

socks, and chestnut-brown leather shoes. She also carried a matching leather shoulder bag.

"It's Alexa the Fashion Reporter Fairy!" Rachel whispered.

Ice Blue Is Cool!

"Girls, I need to talk to you!" Alexa whispered, glancing over at Mr. Walker anxiously.

"Let's hide behind the tree," Kirsty suggested.

They all darted behind the tree, out of sight, and Alexa breathed a sigh of relief.

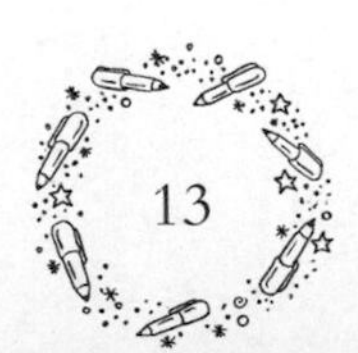

"I'm so glad to see you girls," she declared. "I need your help to get my magic pen back from Jack Frost and his goblins!"

"Look at this, Alexa." Rachel showed her the Ice Blue flyer. "My dad found it in his newspaper."

Alexa nodded sadly. "Jack Frost is using the magic of my special pen to tell everyone about his crazy Ice Blue outfits," she explained. "I need my pen so that I can let everyone know about all the different styles of fashion. Then they can choose to wear what works best for them. If we don't find the pen soon, everyone will be wearing only Ice Blue clothes!"

"Let's go and look for it," Kirsty suggested.

Alexa jumped into Rachel's pocket, and the girls hurried out from behind the tree.

"Dad, can we go to the mall for a little while?" Rachel asked.

Her father looked up from his newspaper and nodded. "I'll meet you by the press booth in about half an hour," he told them.

The girls headed to the mall entrance. As they approached

the doors, they saw a woman on a bicycle pedaling furiously past them. She was red in the face, and her long black hair was flying out behind her.

"She's in a hurry!" Rachel murmured.

The woman jumped off her bike, rested it on its stand, and yanked her purse out of the wicker basket on the front of the bike. But then the purse fell open, and everything spilled on the ground.

"Oh, no!" The woman groaned.

Rachel and Kirsty stopped to help and began picking up her notebook, papers, pens, coin purse, and cell phone.

"Thank you so much," the woman said, taking her phone from Rachel. "I've had such an

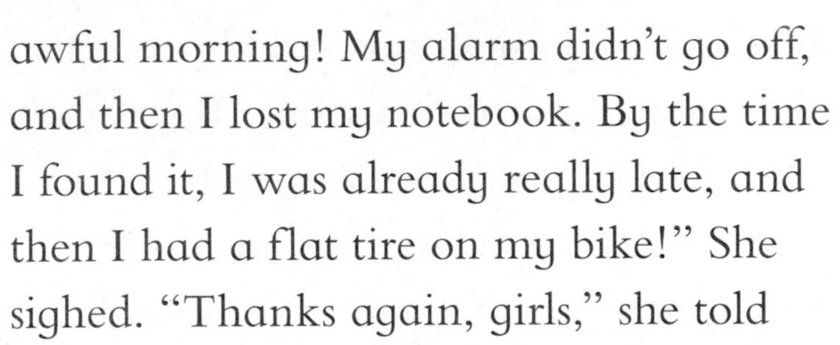

awful morning! My alarm didn't go off, and then I lost my notebook. By the time I found it, I was already really late, and then I had a flat tire on my bike!" She sighed. "Thanks again, girls," she told them. Then, clutching her purse, the woman raced into the mall.

"I wonder who she is and what she's late for." Kirsty remarked as they followed her inside.

Rachel didn't answer. She was staring up at one of the big TV screens that showed advertisements. On the screen, models were posing in weird blue outfits like the ones in the newspaper flyer.

"Ice Blue again!" Rachel said.

The girls glanced around and were dismayed when they realized that all

the TV screens they could see were showing the same advertisement. Not only that, there were announcements every few minutes over the mall's loudspeakers.

"ICE BLUE!" a voice boomed out. "The ONLY clothes for people who love to look COOL!"

"Jack Frost's fashion label is *everywhere*!" Kirsty pointed out, looking worried. As the girls walked through the crowded mall, they could see Ice Blue clothes on display in the windows of all the stores. There were lots of shoppers admiring the clothes, too.

"There must be some people who *don't* like Ice Blue!" Kirsty said. "Maybe we should try to interview shoppers for our magazine. Do you see anyone you know, Rachel?"

Rachel glanced around. "I think most of Tippington is here!" She laughed. "Let's search for Alexa's magic pen, and I'll look for someone we can interview."

The girls walked on, keeping their eyes open for the magic pen. Suddenly, Rachel gasped with excitement. "There's Jodie Allen with her family," she said. "She's in my class at school."

Jodie was with her mom, her younger brother, her teenage sister, and her grandma, and Rachel knew them all. They were peering into one of the store windows at a display of Ice Blue clothes. The girls went over to them.

"Hi, Jodie," Rachel said with a smile. "My friend Kirsty and I are making our own fashion magazine, and we wondered if we could interview you and your family about your favorite design labels."

"Oh, that's easy, Rachel," Jodie said with a big grin. "We all love Ice Blue!"

"*All* of you?" Rachel repeated, shocked.

"Absolutely!" Mrs. Allen agreed. "The clothes are really beautiful and unusual, and they look good on everyone, no matter what age you are."

"What about your other favorite labels?" asked Kirsty.

"We don't like any other clothes now, only Ice Blue," Mrs. Allen told her.

"My friends are all wearing Ice Blue, too," Jodie's sister chimed in. "It's really cool!"

"Even Jake loves Ice Blue," Jodie said, smiling at her little brother, "and he's not into clothes at all!"

"I'm thinking of buying that for myself." Jodie's grandma pointed at a blue coat in the shop window. The coat had extra-long, droopy sleeves, a ragged hem, and buttons stuck all over it. "What do you think?"

"Beautiful!" the rest of Jodie's family announced all at once.

"Thanks for talking to us," Rachel said politely as she and Kirsty moved away.

"They're all crazy about Ice Blue!" Kirsty murmured to her friend. "This is terrible."

Alexa peeked out of Rachel's pocket. "And it'll get worse unless we find my pen!" she told them.

The girls walked past various shops, including Pens 'n' Paper Stationery, Hartley's Department Store, and Fashion First. Then they spotted a crowd of people gathered ahead of them. They were all gazing at a giant TV screen, the biggest in the mall.

"Oh, look!" Kirsty exclaimed, recognizing the face that had just flashed up on the screen. "That's Ella McCauley!" The girls had met Ella, a well-known fashion designer, at the workshop the day before. Rachel and Kirsty had liked her very much, and they also loved the fun, casual clothes that she designed.

"Read an exclusive interview with Ella McCauley in the upcoming edition of *The Fountains Fashion News*!" the voice-over said.

Alexa peeked out of Rachel's pocket. "At last!" she whispered with a grin. "Something that *isn't* about Ice Blue!"

The advertisement changed, and another face appeared on the screen.

It was a woman with long black hair. Kirsty and Rachel recognized her immediately.

"It's the woman who was on the bicycle!" Kirsty murmured.

"Welcome to Fountains Fashion TV," the woman said with a smile. "I'm your fashion reporter, Nicki Anderson, and today we're here live in the mall to talk about the fashion label that's taking the world by storm — Ice Blue!"

The girls glanced at each other in dismay.

"And I have one of the Ice Blue models here with me right now," Nicki continued.

The camera moved off Nicki and onto the person standing next to her. Rachel and Kirsty could hardly believe their eyes when they saw a goblin smirking at the camera!

Nicki Needs Help

The goblin was wearing a patchwork jacket and pants, both made from squares of material in different shades of blue. The crowd of people watching the TV went crazy, cheering and clapping as the goblin paraded up and down.

"You look fabulous!" Nicki told the

goblin. "Tell me, why are Ice Blue clothes so popular?"

"Because everyone wants to look as handsome, cool, and fashionable as I do," the goblin replied. "And you don't have to be green like me to look good in Ice Blue clothes!"

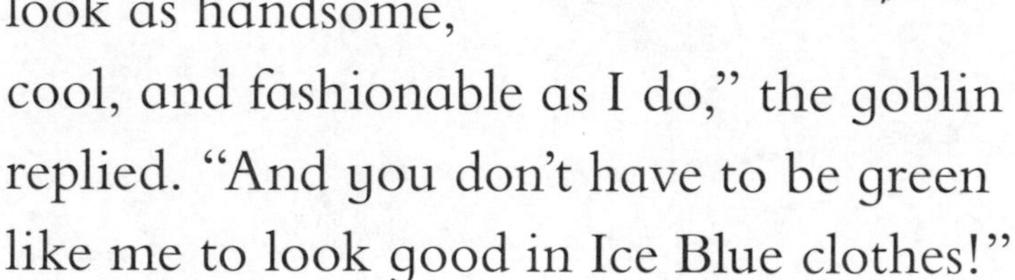

The audience roared with laughter.

"And why *are* you green?" asked Nicki.

"It's face paint," the goblin explained quickly. "Very trendy!"

Rachel and Kirsty watched along with everyone else as more goblins appeared on the screen, modeling other outrageous blue outfits. The watching crowd oohed and aahed, and applauded loudly.

"I want one of those patchwork suits!" Rachel heard a boy say to his friend.

"Me, too," his friend replied. "I love Ice Blue."

Meanwhile, Kirsty was staring hard at the TV. "Look, Rachel," she murmured. The goblins were twirling around, showing off their outfits and then scurrying into the store in the background behind Nicki Anderson. "I recognize that store — it's Pens 'n' Paper."

"That would be a great place to hide my magic pen!" Alexa whispered.

"Let's go!" said Rachel.

The girls scurried across the mall, back to the Pens 'n' Paper shop they'd passed earlier. They arrived just in time to catch Nicki Anderson ending her live report.

"And that's all from me for now," Nicki said to the camera. She was now wearing an Ice Blue baseball cap with a logo of Jack Frost on the front. "Just remember — Ice Blue is the fashion label of the future!"

Nicki handed her microphone to the cameraman, then noticed the girls.

"Hi again," she said warmly. "Thanks for helping me this morning. Sorry I can't stay and chat, but I'm supposed to be interviewing Ella McCauley now for *The Fountains Fashion News*. Can you tell me what time it is?"

"Quarter after eleven," Rachel told her.

Nicki looked shocked. "Oh, no! I'm fifteen minutes late!" she exclaimed. "I was on my way to meet Ella, but I got cornered by the Ice Blue crew! Girls, could you help me carry my things to the press booth? Maybe Ella is waiting for me there."

"Of course," said Rachel.

Nicki picked up her purse and handed Kirsty her coat and Rachel her big notebook. Then the three of them ran through the crowd of shoppers to the press booth.

"Have you seen Ella McCauley?" Nicki asked the

woman in the booth. "I'm late for an interview with her."

"Ella *was* here," the woman replied, "but she went outside into the park to be interviewed by another reporter."

"Oh, no!" Nicki sighed. "I hope Ella has time to talk to me afterward because I really need that interview! I'd better call my boss and tell her what's happening."

"Why don't we go outside and look for Ella?" asked Kirsty helpfully.

"Oh, would you?" Nicki said, taking out her phone. "That would be great!"

Rachel and Kirsty hurried out of the mall.

"Nicki's having lots of bad luck because my magic pen is missing!" Alexa said solemnly. "It's very nice of you to help her, girls."

"I hope Nicki doesn't get into trouble with her boss," Rachel remarked. She stopped and gazed around the huge gardens. "I wonder where Ella is."

"It would be easier to spot her if we could fly," Kirsty suggested.

"That's just what I was going to say!"

Alexa replied with a grin. They all ducked behind a bush that was cut into the shape of a swan. Then Alexa zoomed out of Rachel's pocket and hovered above the girls. With a sprinkle of magic fairy dust from her wand, Rachel and Kirsty became fairy-size.

The three friends whirled up into the air and began to search the gardens. They flew over the tops of the autumn trees and the lake, but there was no sign of Ella. After a while,

Rachel finally spotted a fancy red-and-gold bandstand, half hidden by the trees.

"I can see Ella!" Rachel announced to Kirsty and Alexa. "She's sitting in the bandstand with the other reporter."

As they flew closer, Rachel could see that Ella was showing her sketchbook and some fabric samples to the interviewer. But then Kirsty noticed the actual reporter. He was wearing an Ice Blue patchwork suit and enormous blue shoes.

"He's a goblin!" Kirsty realized. And clutched in the goblin's big green hand was Alexa's magic pen!

Furious Jack Frost

Quickly, Kirsty pointed out the goblin with the pen to Rachel and Alexa.

"We have to get it back!" Rachel insisted as the three fairies landed on the bandstand roof.

Alexa put a finger to her lips. "Let's listen to what the goblin's saying," she whispered. "We need to think of a plan

to grab my pen, but we'll have to wait until he's done interviewing Ella."

"Your fashion designs are OK," the goblin was telling Ella, "but they look ridiculous with all those colors!

The clothes would be much better if they were all in shades of blue."

"I like blue, but I prefer to use lots of different colors," Ella replied politely.

"Huh!" the goblin snorted with disgust. "That's nonsense! Blue is the best color in the whole world! Why don't you join the Ice Blue team and work for us? After all, we're creating the fashion of the future!"

Rachel and Kirsty shook their heads as they looked at each other.

"Isn't he rude?" Rachel said in a low voice. "Ella's designs are beautiful *and* comfortable — not like Ice Blue!"

"Poor Ella," Kirsty sighed. "She's very polite, but she must be a little annoyed." Then her face lit up. "Oh — I have an idea!" Kirsty exclaimed. "But I need to be my human size again."

Quickly, the three friends flew down from the bandstand and fluttered behind a tree. A stream of glittery sparkles from Alexa's wand made

Kirsty shoot up to her usual size. Then she headed toward the bandstand.

"Sorry to interrupt," Kirsty called as she went up the steps. "But the mall reporter, Nicki, is waiting for Ella at the press booth."

The goblin glared at Kirsty, but Ella jumped to her feet immediately. Kirsty could see that she looked very relieved.

"Thank you, Kirsty," Ella said. She smiled at the goblin. "And thank you for interviewing me."

The goblin didn't smile back. "You can't go yet!" he protested. But Ella had already hurried down the steps.

Instantly, Rachel and Alexa swooped onto the bandstand. When the goblin saw them, he shrieked with rage.

"Pesky fairies!" he hollered. He raced for the steps to escape, but Kirsty blocked his way.

"We'd like Alexa's magic pen back, please," Kirsty said firmly.

"Never!" the goblin yelled. Rachel and Alexa fluttered around his head, trying to distract him, and the goblin frantically swatted at them.

Meanwhile, Kirsty tried to grab the pen, but the goblin kept spinning out of her reach.

"HEY!" An angry shout made them all stop and look around. To Kirsty's horror, she saw Jack Frost striding across the garden toward them. He was wearing an Ice Blue suit. Like Ella, he carried a portfolio and a book of fabric samples.

"It's Jack Frost!" Kirsty gasped, turning to Rachel and Alexa. "Quick — hide!"

Rachel and Alexa zoomed back to the top of the bandstand and out of sight. The goblin burst out laughing.

"Not very brave now, are you?" he jeered, still tightly clutching Alexa's pen.

Jack Frost stomped up the bandstand steps. He looked very angry! But Kirsty was surprised to see that Jack Frost wasn't staring at *her* — instead he was glaring furiously at the goblin.

"What are you doing?" he roared.

The goblin jumped with fright. "Um — er — I was just interviewing —" he began.

"Why are you using the magic pen to interview this silly designer?" Jack Frost demanded, pointing at Kirsty. "You're supposed to be interviewing *me* about Ice Blue!" He turned to Kirsty. "Time for you to go!" he snapped.

Kirsty hurried down the steps and hid behind a nearby tree, where she could see and hear everything that was going on. Rachel and Alexa rushed to join her.

"If you can't do
the job right,
I'll do it
myself!"
Jack Frost
told the goblin.
He pointed his
wand and unleashed

a bolt of icy magic. Alexa's pen flew out of the goblin's hand and into Jack Frost's jacket pocket!

Kirsty, Rachel, and Alexa glanced at one another in silent fear. How were they going to get the pen back *now*?

Who Has a Pen?

Jack Frost impatiently waved the goblin away. The goblin trudged off, kicking gloomily at piles of autumn leaves. Meanwhile, Jack Frost sat down on the bandstand steps. He took out the pen and an ice-blue notebook, and cleared his throat.

"So, Mr. Frost, you're clearly a very

talented fellow!" Jack Frost said in a deep, admiring tone. "May we see your wonderful portfolio and fabric samples?" Then he slid across to the opposite side of the step. "Of course you can," Jack Frost said in his normal voice. Smiling boastfully, he opened his portfolio. "As you can see, all my designs have the Jack Frost silhouette logo."

"Jack Frost is interviewing himself!" Kirsty whispered. She, Rachel, and Alexa tried not to laugh.

"These are truly remarkable designs, Mr. Frost," Jack Frost went on, swapping seats again. "What is your inspiration for Ice Blue?"

He slid back across the step.

"Well, *me*, really," Jack Frost replied with a smug grin. "I'm so handsome, I inspire myself!"

"Jack Frost just gave me an idea," Rachel murmured. "I think I know how we can get the pen back! Alexa, will you make me human-size again?"

"Of course," Alexa agreed.

"But I have to be dressed in Ice Blue clothes!" Rachel told her.

Kirsty watched as a burst of Alexa's fairy magic turned Rachel back to her normal size. But now she was wearing a crazy Ice Blue outfit — pants covered with diamond-shaped blue patches and an enormous baggy T-shirt with the Jack Frost logo on it. Kirsty couldn't help laughing.

Rachel grinned at her. "It's your turn, Kirsty!" she declared.

Alexa waved her wand. Now Kirsty was also dressed from head to toe in a weird blue outfit — a backward jacket, clown pants, and a baseball cap with an enormous bill. This time, it was Rachel's turn to burst out laughing. Then she quickly whispered her plan to Alexa and Kirsty. They nodded, and Alexa flew to hide under the bill of Kirsty's hat.

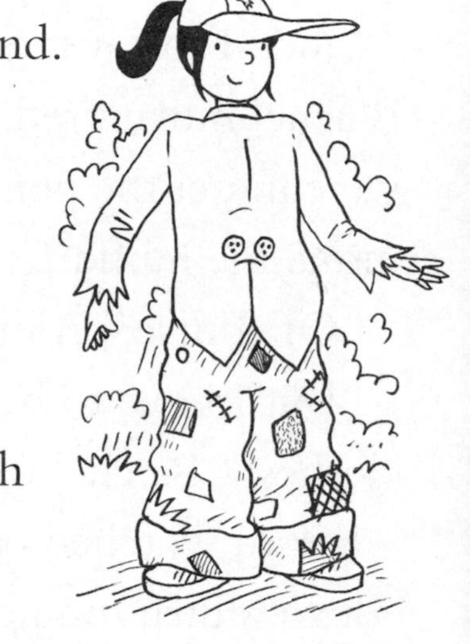

Quickly, the girls hurried out from behind the tree.

"Look!" Rachel yelled, sounding breathless with excitement. "There's the famous designer who makes all of these amazing Ice Blue clothes!"

Jack Frost heard her and peered at them.

"Oh, yes!" said Kirsty. "Let's go tell him how much we *love* his fabulous outfits!"

The girls rushed over to the bandstand. Jack Frost jumped to his feet and greeted them with a gracious smile. "I can see you're fans of my designer label," he said, looking thrilled.

"You've got great taste and style!" Kirsty gushed.

"We threw all our other clothes away," Rachel told him.

"We're only going to wear Ice Blue from now on!" added Kirsty.

Jack Frost nodded. "Soon everyone in the whole world will be wearing Ice Blue," he replied proudly. "I'm doing an interview to spread the word about my designs."

Rachel and Kirsty glanced around the bandstand.

"But where's the reporter?" Kirsty asked.

"I'm interviewing myself," Jack Frost explained. He sighed. "But it's not easy."

"Maybe *we* could interview you?" Rachel suggested. "It would be such an honor!"

"We can tell everyone how great Ice Blue is," said Kirsty.

"That's a good idea," Jack Frost replied with a smug smile. "But I'll only do the interview if I can tell you what questions to ask."

"OK," Rachel agreed. She turned to Kirsty. "Do you have a pen?" Rachel asked her.

Kirsty shook her head. "Sorry."

"I don't have one, either." Rachel frowned. She looked at Jack Frost. "Could we borrow *your* pen?"

Jack Frost hesitated. Rachel waited for his answer, hoping she didn't look too nervous. Would her plan work?

Jack Frost scowled.

"Well," he muttered reluctantly, "I guess so. But I want it back as soon as you're finished with the interview."

He handed the pen over to Rachel, who sighed with relief. At that moment, Alexa swooped out from under Kirsty's baseball cap and zoomed over to Rachel.

Jack Frost gave a shout of rage, but it all happened too fast for him to do anything. The instant Alexa touched the pen, it shrank to its Fairyland size, and she tucked it safely away inside her bag.

"You think you're so smart!" Jack Frost sneered, stomping his foot. "But you won't stop me! I still have three of the Fashion Fairies' magical objects left, and soon my Ice Blue clothes will take over the world!" He stormed off in a rage.

"Girls, I can't thank you enough."

Alexa smiled at Rachel and Kirsty. "To show you just how grateful I am, let me change your terrible clothes!" She pointed her wand at Rachel and Kirsty. In an instant, the two girls were back in the clothes they'd been wearing earlier.

"Thanks, Alexa," Kirsty said with a grin. "I could hardly see where I was going in that huge baseball cap!"

"I have to rush back to Fairyland and share the good news with everyone," Alexa said happily. "Now fashion reporters everywhere will be able to tell people about *all* the wonderful clothes they can buy, not just Ice Blue. Good-bye, girls. I'd love to see your fashion magazine when it's finished!" Then Alexa vanished in a mist of sparkling fairy dust.

"That was close!" Kirsty sighed as she and Rachel hurried back into the mall. "I didn't think Jack Frost was going to let us borrow Alexa's pen!"

"Me, neither," Rachel agreed. "We better go straight to the press booth. It's time to meet my dad."

"I wonder if Nicki got her interview with Ella after all." Kirsty said.

When the girls reached the press booth, they saw that Nicki was in the middle of interviewing Ella. They were surrounded by a crowd of people. Mr. Walker was up in front, so Rachel and Kirsty went to join him.

"What do you think about this new Ice Blue label?" Nicki was asking Ella.

"Well, the designer has some very unusual ideas," Ella replied carefully, "but the color blue doesn't suit *everyone*.

I always think it's best to let people choose what they want to wear

depending on what looks best on them."

Nicki nodded. "And can you tell us about the design competition you were involved in yesterday?" she said.

"We were looking for wonderful outfits for the charity fashion show at the end of this week," Ella explained. "We wanted original designs with imagination and flair." Just then, she spotted Rachel and Kirsty at the front of the crowd. "Would you like to interview two of the winners, Nicki?" Ella motioned for the girls to come forward.

The audience applauded as Rachel and Kirsty joined Nicki and Ella. Mr. Walker looked on proudly.

"So, girls, how does it feel to be competition winners?" Nicki asked with a smile.

"Great!" said Kirsty, feeling a little shy.

"Fantastic!" Rachel added.

"Tell us about your designs," Nicki went on.

Rachel briefly described her rainbow

jeans, and Kirsty talked about her scarf dress. Nicki and the audience all looked very interested.

"Thank you, girls," Nicki told them. "We look forward to seeing you model your outfits at the charity fashion show later this week!"

As the audience applauded, Rachel and Kirsty smiled at each other. They were both thrilled that they'd already found four of the Fashion Fairies' magical objects! But the girls knew

that the charity fashion show would be a disaster unless they found the last three objects and returned them safely to the Fashion Fairies. Everything to do with fashion in the human and fairy worlds would be ruined! They still had some exciting adventures to come!

Kirsty and Rachel tracked down
Alexa's magic pen.
Now it's time for them to help

Jennifer
the Hairstylist Fairy!

Read on for a sneak peek. . . .

Kirsty Tate and her best friend, Rachel Walker, gazed into the salon mirrors with excitement. They were sitting side by side, waiting to have their hair cut in the coolest salon in town — Snip & Clip.

"What's it going to be, girls?" asked Blair, the head hairstylist.

"I just want a trim," said Kirsty.

"What about you, Rachel?" asked Claire, the other stylist. "Are you going to try something more daring?"

Rachel's eyes sparkled as she looked at Claire in the mirror.

"I'd really love to have lots of tiny braids all over my head," she said. "Could you do that?"

"There's nothing that Claire can't do with hair!" said Blair with a laugh. "Let's get started."

The girls looked down at the cart that stood between them. It was full of special hairdressing scissors, combs, and brushes, pretty barrettes, headbands, and jewels. They looked up and smiled at each other.

"I love getting my hair done," said Rachel. "It's even more fun when you're here with me!"

Kirsty was spending the fall break in Tippington with Rachel. As a special treat, Mrs. Walker had brought them to the new salon in the Tippington Fountains Shopping Center. Mrs. Walker was reading a magazine in the waiting area. She was planning to have her hair styled for a party that she and Mr. Walker were going to that night.

"Tippington Fountains is the best shopping mall ever," said Kirsty. "We're so lucky — we've visited every single day since it opened!"

SPECIAL EDITION

Three Books in Each One— More Rainbow Magic Fun!

Joy the Summer Vacation Fairy
Holly the Christmas Fairy
Kylie the Carnival Fairy
Stella the Star Fairy
Shannon the Ocean Fairy
Trixie the Halloween Fairy
Gabriella the Snow Kingdom Fairy
Juliet the Valentine Fairy
Mia the Bridesmaid Fairy
Flora the Dress-Up Fairy
Paige the Christmas Play Fairy
Emma the Easter Fairy
Cara the Camp Fairy
Destiny the Rock Star Fairy
Belle the Birthday Fairy
Olympia the Games Fairy
Selena the Sleepover Fairy
Cheryl the Christmas Tree Fairy
Florence the Friendship Fairy
Lindsay the Luck Fairy

scholastic.com
rainbowmagiconline.com

HIT entertainment
RMSPECIAL10